Flump Chump

FLUMP CHUMP

Published by Mialand Adventures
www.mialandadventures.com

Illustrated by Eric Splodge
Book design by www.truenorthpublish.com

ISBN 978-0615932514
Printed in the United States of America.

Flump Chump

by MIA HUBBARD

Illustrated by Eric Splodge

MIALAND ADVENTURES

Acknowledgements

Many thanks to my Family and Friends,
who have listened time and time again to the story of Flump Chump.
Thanks especially to Phill Moon, who has encouraged
and developed my creative abilities,
Brian Del Turco, who published this book for me
and finally thanks to my own, little Flump Chump...Bradley Houston.

This is a story about a creature like no other.

His name was Flump Chump and it was said
he was the last of his kind.
With his spiky fur, big antlers and long, windy tail,
Flump Chump had a look all of his own.

But unfortunately his unusual looks
also meant he didn't quite fit in.
So poor old Flump Chump used to stay deep in the
woods, often finding caves to stay in
and trees to hide amongst.

Now before we go on,
there is something else important to tell you
about Flump Chump.

He had, if you like, special powers.
His fur and his antlers and even his tail
would change colour depending on his mood;
so when he was sad he was blue,
when he was shy he went red
and when he was happy he was yellow.

As the years went by without anyone to talk to,
Flump Chump got more and more lonely,
which meant most of the time his fur was blue.
There were times when he wouldn't
change colour for months on end!

He tried speaking to the trees and the flowers
but for some reason they didn't want to talk back.
So, the blue little creature hid in the caves,
and stayed quiet to the world.

Flump Chump had a pouch for his heart
and when he slept he took it out of his pouch
and hugged it in his big, furry, hands.

One day though, he noticed that
there was a huge, horrible streak
down the middle of his heart; it was breaking!
With a tear in his eye, Flump Chump
decided it was time for things to change;
he needed a friend.

The next morning Flump Chump
woke up with a smile on his face;
this was the day he would make a friend.
His fur beamed bright yellow
and for the first time in a very long time
he felt happy.

So, with a tasty treat of honey
and marshmallows to eat along the way,
Flump Chump left his cave and ventured
deep into the woods.

Everyday he saw lots of other animals
roaming around in the woods,
but normally he was too shy
to approach them so he just ran away.
Today though, was different;
he was determined!

The first thing Flump Chump saw
was the back of Miss Rabbit's head;
she was intensely focused on eating away
at some delicious dandelion leaves.
This made Flump Chump's stomach rumble,
and he decided to have a quick snack himself.

"I need to be full of energy
if I'm going to try and make a friend",
he muttered to himself.

Flump Chump slowly approached Miss Rabbit and gave a low grunt, "em, excuse me..." he said, clearing his throat.

It took Miss Rabbit a moment to answer, because eating dandelions has always being a very time-consuming, delicious activity.

"Yes?" she said, finally turning around.

"I was just wondering..." Flump Chump began,
and then his hands started to shake nervously.

He was a very shy creature indeed
and at the sight of Miss Rabbit's pretty,
long eyelashes and lovely, blue eyes
he started to blush.

Oh no! It was about to happen.
He suddenly puffed out like a pufferfish
and became bright red.
Why did he have to be so shy?
Miss Rabbit ran away, scared at the sight of him.

Flump Chump watched her
running away with a sad face.
He hated being shy.
Why did all the other animals
think he was so scary?

Flump Chump made his mouth
into a little 'o' shape and started blowing out the air
that had puffed up his belly.
It was like deflating a balloon!
Finally he got back to his normal self,
deciding that he would try again tomorrow
to make a friend.

The next day he woke up with blue,
sad fur and then he remembered;
he was going to make a friend today!
His fur shined a light yellow,
happy at the thought.

"I know," Flump Chump said to himself,
"I'll go down to the river,
I've seen Mr. Otto bathing there
many times before.
Maybe he'll be my friend?"

So off Flump Chump went, singing a song to himself.
He had a beautiful voice, but he only ever sang
when he was feeling happy.
Which was hardly any of the time at all.

Down by the river,
Flump Chump paddled into the water,
looking out for Mr. Otto.
He waited so long
that his stomach started rumbling.
He was always hungry!

He'd forgotten to bring some tasty treats with him,
so he decided he'd try eating the leaves by the water
like Miss Rabbit always did.

Errghhh! They were disgusting. Yak!
How could she eat this!
Flump Chump spat them back out,
patting his rumbling stomach.

"It's okay, I'll get you a toffee apple
when we get home..." he told his belly.

Just when Flump Chump was about to give up,
he saw Mr. Otto swimming towards him.

"Mr. Otto!" Flump Chump called out.

Mr. Otto didn't answer.
He had disappeared deep in the water all of a sudden.
Flump Chump sadly shrugged his shoulders,
preparing to go home.

"Hello what can I get you my dear Mr...
whatever you are!"

Flump Chump jumped into the air
at the sound of Mr. Otto's voice;
he'd snuck up behind him!
Caught off guard, Flump Chump
tried to compose himself.

"Hi, hello, Mr., err, Mr. Otto,
I was just, just wondering, er, if...."

"Well come along and say it old chap,
I haven't got all day."

Flump Chump was suddenly embarrassed.
And when he got embarrassed,
he...OH NO!
He blew up like a balloon.

"Ouch, that hurt,
how dare you spike me you, you, mean, nasty..."
Mr. Otto declared!

"I'm sorry I didn't mean to..."
Flump Chump began
but Mr. Otto had already swam away.

Out he blew the air that filled up his belly,
watching with tears in his eyes
as Mr. Otto went away.
Poor Flump Chump's fur
turned blue and home he went.

That night as Flump Chump slept
with his heart in his hands,
it cracked right down the middle,
falling into two separate pieces.

Flump Chump awoke with a shock;
oh no, his heart had broken!
He got some glue and tried to fix it together,
but the glue wasn't strong enough
and it just kept breaking apart.
So next he got some sticky-tape
but that didn't work either!

"I know," Flump Chump muttered,
"there's only one thing for this!"

He got out some honey, it had a nice,
sticky texture that would easily fix the problem.
And that it did.
Flump Chump smiled to himself.

"Good work," he told himself
and decided he'd treat himself to the rest
of the honey pot to celebrate.

Flump Chump knew that to keep his heart stuck together
he would have to make a friend very soon.

The next day, Flump Chump got up
but this time he wasn't bright yellow.
He wasn't as sure he would make a friend
and unfortunately his fur stayed blue and sad.

He walked into the woods
but on his way tripped over a log.

"Ouch," a little voice said.

Flump Chump looked behind him
and realised it wasn't a log he had tripped over,
it was a mole!

"Oh I'm so sorry," Flump Chump said.

"It's okay, I'm okay."

The little mole staggered to his feet,
dusting the mud away.

"I'm so, so sorry,"
Flump Chump said again,
he couldn't believe he had managed to hurt someone.

No matter what he did,
it seemed he would only ever scare and hurt people.
Maybe he should just live in a cave forever
and hide himself away.

"Like I said, it's okay, you couldn't help it!"
the little mole brightly declared.
He smiled at Flump Chump,
a big grin on his face.

"Where are you going, my friend?"
the little mole asked.

Flump Chump was shocked, 'friend?'
He hadn't expected that.
Suddenly he felt shy, really shy...OH NO!
Before he knew it he was a big pufferfish,
rolling on the floor.

He was about to cry when he realised
the little mole hadn't ran away.

"Why aren't you running?" Flump Chump asked,
staring at the little mole who was still stood smiling.

"Running?
Why would I be running, my friend?"

Flump Chump blushed again, "because,
because...I'm scary."

"Scary? You don't sound so scary to me!"

"But can't you see," Flump Chump insisted,
"I'm simply horrible!"

"I'll let you in on a little secret,"
the little mole said, coming closer to Flump Chump,
"us moles can't see.
We're born blind, believe it or not.
But like I said, you don't sound so scary to me!"

"Oh." Flump Chump said,
he couldn't quite believe what he was hearing.
"Well in that case..." he said, mustering up his courage,
"would you like to be my friend?"

"Like to? I'd love to," the little mole said,
"I was getting lonely in my little hole myself."

"You were?" Flump Chump said,
"I didn't know other animals got lonely?"

"Of course they do. Everyone gets lonely
at some point."

"They do?"

"Yes. And everyone's a little bit shy, but that's okay.
I've met a lot of animals
and they all sound the same, you know?
Everyone has a similar story."

"Oh." Flump Chump said,
and suddenly he didn't feel so very shy anymore.
He blew out the air, and found himself
shining a bright yellow colour!

He had a new friend and a new confidence too.
He realised that the other animals
were just as shy as he was.
There was no need to get embarrassed.

That night, when Flump Chump
was about to go to sleep,
he took his heart into his hands.

And then he found something miraculous;
it wasn't the same heart at all.
It was a new heart; a happy, yellow-coloured one.
It burnt bright like the sun, and glowed in his hands.

Flump Chump put it back in his pouch,
and when he did so something amazing happened;
the heart sank through into his fur
and glowed from the inside.

Flump Chump smiled,
knowing no one would ever be able
to steal his happiness again.

About the Author

Ever since hand-writing her first children's book at the age of seven, Mia Hubbard has had a keen passion for creative writing. Told by family and friends that she often lives in her 'own little world' she has always had an imaginative mind. Recently having graduated from university, completing a degree in 'English with Creative Writing', Mia Hubbard is currently working for an international charity in the communications and PR department. Working on her latest series of children's books, Mia hopes that her stories will both inspire and bring laughter to her readers, both children and parents alike!

About Flump Chump ...
'I didn't know other animals got lonely.'
'Of course they do. Everyone gets lonely at some point.'
Flump Chump finds more than a best friend when he meets Little Mole. What his new friend teaches him will change him forever.

Often told that I have a childlike sense of wonder, I have never lost the excitement that a child feels when viewing the world. I aim to give children the tools necessary to deal with the trials and tribulations that life sometimes brings, and show that although things can seem tough, there are always positives to be found along every journey!

I am currently working on a series of children's books, full of strange, little creatures who participate in a range of exciting adventures. I hope to publish more in the near future, and look forward to introducing these timid, little characters to the big ol' world.

I am also interested in writing stories for adults, and aim to finish my first novel.

www.mialandadventures.com